GREAT ILLUSTRATED CLASSICS

THE THREE MUSKETEERS

Alexandre Dumas

**adapted by
Malvina G. Vogel**

**Illustrations by
Pablo Marcos Studio**

ABDO
Publishing Company

GREAT ILLUSTRATED CLASSICS

edited by
Malvina G. Vogel

visit us at
www.abdopub.com

Library editions published in 2002 by ABDO Publishing Company, 4940 Viking Drive, Suite 622, Edina, Minnesota 55435. Published by agreement with Playmore Incorporated Publishers and Waldman Publishing Corporation.

Library of Congress Cataloging-in-Publication Data

Dumas, Alexander, 1802-1870.
   The three musketeers / Alexander Dumas; adapted by Malvina G. Vogel; Illustrated by Pablo Marcos Studio.
      p. cm – (Great illustrated classics)
   Reprint. Originally published: New York: Playmore: Waldman Pub., 1990.
   Summary: In seventeenth-century France, young D'Artagnan initially quarrels with, then befriends, three musketeers and joins them in trying to outwit the enemies of the king and queen.
   ISBN 1-57765-803-5
   1. France–History–Louis XIII, 1610-1643–Juvenile fiction. [1. France–History–Louis XIII, 1610-1643--Fiction. 2. Adventure and adventurers–Fiction.] I. Vogel, Malvina G. II. Title. III. Series.

PZ7.D893 Th 2002
[Fic]–dc21

2001056486

CONTENTS

About the Author

The year was 1807. Five-year-old Alexandre Dumas knew that he was different from the other boys in the small town of Villers-Cotterêts. For Alexandre was half black and half white. And nobody ever let him forget that.

Education bored young Alexandre, and as he grew, he preferred spending his time hunting and leading an outdoor life. But when Alexandre turned sixteen, his whole life changed. He saw his first play—a performance of Shakespeare's *Hamlet*, and from that moment on, his dream was to go to Paris and become a playwright.

Dumas worked for years as a clerk and wrote in his spare time. He had success writing plays and travel books. But it wasn't until 1844 that Alexandre Dumas hit upon the one kind of story that was to make him rich and famous. That was the historical novel.

In his many historical novels, Dumas took people who really existed in French history and events that actually happened. He added main characters from his own imagination and created entertaining and amusing adventure stories around them.

The most famous of all Dumas' historical novels are *The Three Musketeers, The Count of Monte Cristo,* and *The Man in the Iron Mask.*

Alexandre Dumas wrote more than six hundred books in his lifetime, more than any other man, living or dead. And he made money from them. But he spent everything he earned building elegant mansions, entertaining great artists and writers of Paris, buying theatres and newspapers, and romancing many women.

The man who made the world rich with all his books died in 1870—penniless!

D'Artagnan, the Bold Gascon

Chapter 1
D'Artagnan

The young man riding into the small French town of Meung that April morning in 1625 made the citizens stop their work and stare in amazement. The man had to be from Gascony in southern France. For only a Gascon would have the boldness to be seen on such an old, ridiculous-looking pony. It had a yellowy-orange coat and a tail with no hair. It seemed so ashamed of its appearance that it walked with its head lower than its knees.

But young D'Artagnan of Gascony sat on its back proudly. He was on his way to Paris to join the King's Musketeers—those bold, courageous soldiers who guarded King Louis XIII of France.

D'Artagnan carried with him three gifts from his father: a purse containing fifteen crowns of gold, a sword which had been in his family for generations, and a letter of introduction to Monsieur de Tréville, the Captain of the King's Musketeers.

But D'Artagnan also carried with him his father's parting words. "My son," he had said, "I have taught you how to handle a sword well. You must never draw back from a duel. You must be brave for two reasons—you are a Gascon and you are my son!"

His father's words still rang in his ears as D'Artagnan climbed down from his pony at the Inn of the Jolly Miller in Meung. Three men standing at the front door glanced at him, then looked back a second time. All three burst into laughter.

"I say, sir," said D'Artagnan, approaching

A Father's Gifts

the men, "tell me what you are laughing at. and we will laugh together."

The tallest of the three, a dark-haired nobleman with a patch over one eye and a scar on his cheek, looked from the pony to its master. "I am not speaking to you, sir," he said with a sneer.

"But I am speaking to you!" cried D'Artagnan angrily.

The nobleman ignored D'Artagnan, but pointed to the pony and whispered something to his friends. All three laughed again.

D'Artagnan drew his sword and cried, "Gentlemen, you laugh at a pony, but do you dare laugh at its master?"

"No one tells me when to laugh," said the nobleman. "I laugh when I please." With that, he turned to enter the inn.

But D'Artagnan was not the sort of man to let someone laugh at him and escape. He ran after the man shouting, "Turn around, sir, or

The Strangers Laugh at the Pony.

I shall strike you from behind!"

The man whirled around and drew his sword. But, at the same moment, his two friends came at D'Artagnan with sticks and shovels. One heavy blow opened a large gash in his head and another knocked him unconscious.

The innkeeper sent two of his servants to carry the wounded young man inside. As they placed him on the bed, a letter fell out of his pocket. The innkeeper picked it up and saw that it was addressed to the Captain of the Musketeers.

"Perhaps the nobleman outside would be interested in this," he murmured.

And the nobleman was! "What business can that boy have with my enemy?" he exclaimed in surprise. "Hmm! Well, my business here with Milady is more important right now. I shall look into this letter later."

Meanwhile, D'Artagnan had regained

An Interesting Letter

consciousness and staggered to the door. He saw the nobleman talking to a beautiful young woman seated in an elegant carriage. The man's words reached D'Artagnan's ears.

"The Cardinal has ordered you to return to England at once, Milady. Be at the court often and let him know if the Duke of Buckingham leaves London."

"I understand," replied the woman, "but you must leave quickly too. The least delay, such as that young man, can ruin our plans."

The nobleman leaped on his horse and galloped off in the direction of Paris.

"Come back, coward!" cried D'Artagnan, running out the door. But his wounds had left him too weak to take more than a few steps.

As he stumbled back to the inn, he wondered what the mysterious conversation meant. The Cardinal they had talked about had to be Cardinal Richelieu—the powerful

The Nobleman Gives Milady Her Orders.

man who really ruled France. And the Duke of Buckingham, why he was the Prime Minister of England—the real power behind King Charles I. Was a war being planned between the two countries? He would find out when he reached Paris.

The next morning, as D'Artagnan was dressing to continue his journey, he discovered that his letter to Monsieur de Tréville was missing. He burst in furiously on the innkeeper and demanded to know where it was.

"Oh, Monsieur," said the frightened man, "it was that stranger you challenged to a duel. He stole your letter while you were unconscious."

"The scoundrel! I shall report him to Monsieur de Tréville when I reach Paris."

D'Artagnan rode out of Meung muttering, "He shall be punished! That nobleman with the black patch has not seen the last of D'Artagnan of Gascony!"

D'Artagnan's Letter Is Missing.

A First Look at Real Musketeers

Chapter 2
The Captain of the Musketeers

As D'Artagnan entered the courtyard of Monsieur de Tréville's headquarters, he gazed admiringly at the noisy groups of Musketeers everywhere. Some were practicing their dueling; others were standing in groups, drinking and talking and joking. The jokes seemed to be about the Cardinal's Guards, who were the rivals (and sometimes enemies) of the King's Musketeers.

When D'Artagnan reached the main door of the building, he asked the guard on duty to announce him to Monsieur de Tréville.

Within minutes, the Captain of the

Musketeers came to the door. He motioned for D'Artagnan to go upstairs to his office, then stuck his head out the door, calling loudly, "Athos! Porthos! Aramis!"

Two Musketeers left their group and followed Tréville into the office, passing in front of D'Artagnan, who stood just inside the door. The Musketeers stood at attention while their captain paced back and forth.

Suddenly, Tréville stopped and turned to them angrily. "Gentlemen," he cried, "His Eminence, the Cardinal, has reported to me that three of my men started a riot yesterday in a wine shop, and his guards had to arrest them. Don't deny that it was you, for you were recognized—you, Porthos, you, Aramis, and you....but where is Athos? I called him in here as well."

"Sir," said Aramis sadly, "Athos is ill."

"Wounded, more likely!" said Tréville.

"Well, sir" said Porthos, "there were six

Tréville Scolds Porthos and Aramis.

guards against the three of us. We fought well. Athos, however, was seriously wounded in the chest and right shoulder. But we all managed to escape."

"So, the Cardinal only told me half the story," said Tréville, smiling proudly.

At that moment, the door opened, and all heads turned towards it.

"Athos!" cried Monsieur de Tréville.

"You sent for me, sir," said Athos weakly.

"Yes, my boy! I was about to tell your friends that you are not to risk your lives needlessly. But I'm proud of you all!"

Tréville reached out to shake Athos' hand. He did not notice the murmur of pain that escaped from the brave Musketeer's lips. He was busy congratulating Porthos and Aramis as well.

Once the Musketeers were dismissed, he turned to D'Artagnan. "Now, my boy, what can I do for the son of my oldest friend?"

"Athos!"

"Monsieur," said D'Artagnan, "I had come here to ask to join the Musketeers, but now I don't think I'm worthy of such an honor."

"No one can become a Musketeer until he has performed a great act of courage or until he has served two years in a lower regiment to get his training."

"If only I had my letter of introduction, you'd see that I need no training, sir. But that letter was stolen on my way here."

D'Artagnan then went on to tell Tréville of his adventure at Meung and to describe the stranger who had stolen his letter.

"Tell me, D'Artagnan," said Tréville, "did this man have a scar on his face?"

"Yes, on his right cheek."

"And was the patch over his left eye?"

"Yes, sir. I am certain."

"And did you hear the woman's name?"

"He called her Milady."

"And the instructions he gave her?"

24

Describing the Stranger's Patch

'The Cardinal wished her to return to England and inform him if the Duke of Buckingham left London."

"It is he! It is he!" cried Tréville.

"Oh, sir, please tell me who this man is," pleaded D'Artagnan. "I must have my revenge.

"No! Do not go looking for him ever! Put these ideas of revenge out of your mind, and I shall write a letter admitting you to the regiment I spoke of. You'll make a fine cadet, I'm sure."

Tréville sat down at his desk and began to write. Meanwhile, D'Artagnan strolled over to the window and looked out.

Suddenly, he jumped away and rushed to the door, shouting, "He shall not escape me this time!"

"Who? Who? asked Tréville, startled.

'The man who stole my letter!" cried D'Artagnan as he disappeared out the door.

D'Artagnan Spots the Stranger.

D'Artagnan Runs Headlong into Athos.

Chapter 3
Three Duels

D'Artagnan was in a rage as he bounded down the stairs. He didn't notice the Musketeer on the landing until he ran headlong into him.

"Excuse me!" said D'Artagnan, trying to get by. "I'm in a hurry."

"Just because you are in a hurry," said the Musketeer blocking his way, "is no reason for you to run into me."

"My God!" cried D'Artagnan, recognizing Athos. "I did not hit against your wound on purpose. Now please let me pass."

"I find you quite impolite," said Athos.

"Well, you are hardly one to give me a-lesson in manners"

"Then perhaps a lesson in dueling!"

"I am ready to fight you. Tell me where!"

"Behind the Carmelite Convent at noon."

D'Artagnan nodded and rushed down the stairs and into the courtyard. At the gate to the street stood Porthos and a guard. There seemed to be just enough room between the two men for D'Artagnan to pass through. So he darted into the opening.

But, at that moment, a gust of wind caught the edge of Porthos' cloak and blew it across the opening. D'Artagnan found himself trapped inside the folds of the cloak.

"Good Lord!" cried Porthos. "Are you a madman, running into people like this?"

"Excuse me, sir," said D'Artagnan, gazing up at the giant. "I am in a great hurry."

"And do you forget your eyes when you

Trapped in Porthos' Cloak

run? You deserve to be punished for this!"

"Punished, Monsieur!" cried D'Artagnan. "And who exactly is going to punish me?"

"I, Monsieur!" cried Porthos. "At one o'clock behind the Luxembourg Gardens."

"Very well," said D'Artagnan as he rushed into the street.

He looked around. There was no sign of the stranger in any direction. He ran in and out of the side streets for over an hour, then finally gave up the chase.

"What a crackbrained idiot I am!" he muttered to himself as he walked. "I've been in Paris only three hours, and already I've made a bad impression on Monsieur de Tréville, and I've set up two duels with Musketeers who could easily kill me. If I somehow survive these duels; I must remember to be more polite in the future."

At that moment, he looked up and saw Aramis talking to three guards at the

"What a Crackbrained Idiot I Am!"

courtyard gate. D'Artagnan would not have dreamed of interrupting them if he had not seen Aramis drop his handkerchief and step on it.

Wishing to be of help, D'Artagnan rushed up to him, bent down, and pulled the handkerchief out from under his foot. He held it out to Aramis and, in his most polite voice, said, "I believe, sir, that you have lost your handkerchief."

Aramis turned red and grabbed the lace cloth from D'Artagnan's hand. The scent of its perfume reached the guards.

"Ah ha! Aramis," cried one of the guards. "A lace handkerchief embroidered with a crown. A gift from one of the Queen's ladies-in-waiting, no doubt? Tell us about her."

Realizing that he had embarrassed Aramis, D'Artagnan tried to apologize. "I hope you will excuse me, sir. . . ."

"Excuse you?" cried Aramis. "Any fool

D'Artagnan Returns Aramis' Handkerchief.

should know that a gentleman doesn't step on a lady's handkerchief unless he's hiding it."

"A fool, you say!" shouted D'Artagnan. "I did try to apologize, sir."

"There is only one way to apologize for such an insult," said Aramis. "My sword will be ready at two o'clock behind the church."

"And so will mine," said D'Artagnan.

It was almost noon, and he hurried to keep his appointment with Athos. "Well," he thought, "if I am to be killed today, at least it will be by a Musketeer."

When D'Artagnan reached the bare plot of land behind the convent, he found Athos already there waiting. They greeted each other and Athos said that his seconds would be arriving at any moment.

"I have no seconds, sir," said D'Artagnan "no one to witness the duel for me, for I only arrived in Paris this morning and I know no one. But I shall be honored to cross swords

A Handshake Before a Duel

with a brave Musketeer who fights even though his wounds pain him."

"It does hurt like the devil!" said Athos

"Perhaps then, you will accept a salve I brought from Gascony. My mother makes it herself, and it heals any wound in two days."

"That is very kind of you," said Athos with a smile and a bow. "I have the feeling that if we don't kill each other in this duel, we shall become good friends... Ah, here come my seconds now."

D'Artagnan turned and saw two Musketeers approaching. "Your seconds are Porthos and Aramis?" he cried.

"Why, yes," said Athos. "We are never seen one without the other. All Paris knows us as the Three Musketeers. Our motto is 'One for all and all for one!'"

"What is *he* doing here?" cried Porthos as he came closer and saw D'Artagnan.

"This is the gentleman I am to duel," said

Athos' Seconds Arrive.

Athos.

"But I am to fight him too!" cried Porthos.

"And I, as well," added Aramis.

"Then, Monsieur Athos," said D'Artagnan, "let us begin. I do not wish to keep my other worthy opponents waiting."

The two men drew their swords. But hardly had the swords clicked twice than a group of Cardinal's Guards turned the corner.

"Sheathe your swords quickly!" called Porthos. "They will try to enforce the Cardinal's order against dueling."

But it was too late. The guards approached and ordered them under arrest.

"There are five of them," said Athos quietly, "and we are only three. But I would rather die here than face Monsieur de Tréville defeated by the guards again!"

"Gentlemen," interrupted D'Artagnan, "you are not three; we are four. I may not wear the uniform of a Musketeer, but I have the

The Cardinal's Guards Approach.

heart of one!"

"Well then," cried Athos, "forward!"

"One for all and all for one!" they shouted together as they lunged at the Cardinal's Guards. D'Artagnan fought like a tiger, proud to be dueling alongside the brave Musketeers. Within minutes, they had killed four of the guards and wounded the fifth.

"That is enough," said Athos. "Let us help this wounded man to the steps of the convent and then be on our way."

The Three Musketeers took D'Artagnan's arm, and together they walked along, taking up the whole width of the street. They greeted every Musketeer they met along the way with shouts of "One for all and all for one!" and introduced their new friend.

This was a victory march that filled D'Artagnan's heart with joy. He was on his way to becoming a King's Musketeer!

"One for All and All for One!"

Congratulations from the King

Chapter 4
D'Artagnan's Visitor

When Monsieur de Tréville learned of the defeat of the Cardinal's Guards, he scolded the Musketeers in public, but congratulated them in private. The King, too, was delighted to see Richelieu embarrassed, for although he gave the Cardinal great power, he also enjoyed seeing him suffer defeat as well.

King Louis XIII summoned the four friends to the palace to congratulate them.

"Come in, my brave men," said the King.

D'Artagnan and the Three Musketeers approached their King and bowed.

When Louis saw the young Gascon, he

exclaimed, "Why, you are just a boy! Yet you fought so bravely alongside my Musketeers. I must reward you. Here, take these forty pistoles. Surely you can put them to good use since you are new to Paris."

D'Artagnan took the handful of gold coins and bowed deeply. "Thank you, Sire," he said.

"And now, gentlemen," added the King, "I thank you all for your devotion to me."

Once the men had left the palace, D'Artagnan asked his friends how he should spend his money. Athos suggested that first they all enjoy a good dinner. Porthos then suggested that D'Artagnan hire a lackey—a servant to take care of his needs. And Aramis suggested that he find a place to live.

Once all three had been accomplished, D'Artagnan settled down to the life of a cadet. For several months, he trained enthusiastically and spent all his free time with the Musketeers. Yet, in spite of their close

A Reward for Bravery

friendship, D'Artagnan learned very little about the private lives of the three men.

He knew only that Athos was a nobleman with an unhappy love affair in his past, that Porthos was having a romance with a duchess who wanted to marry him, and that Aramis hoped to become a priest when he left the service of the Musketeers.

As time went on, D'Artagnan did learn, however, that forty pistoles didn't last forever. His pockets were nearly empty when one day his lackey, Planchet, showed in a visitor.

The short, stout man in his fifties looked familiar, but D'Artagnan wasn't sure from where. He greeted the man and asked if he could be of service.

"I know you are a brave cadet, Monsieur D'Artagnan," said the man, "and I always see you with the daring Musketeers. So I feel I can trust you with my secret."

D'Artagnan Has a Visitor.

"Of course, Monsieur! Go on," said D'Artagnan, sensing an adventure on the way.

"Well, Monsieur, I have a young wife who is a lady-in-waiting to the Queen. Yesterday, as my wife was leaving the palace, she was kidnapped."

"Do you have any idea why?"

"Because of love and politics at the court! Because of the love of the...Queen!"

"Queen Anne?" cried D'Artagnan.

"Yes! Everyone in France knows that the poor Queen is ignored by the King and that their marriage was arranged simply to keep peace between France and Spain. But our beautiful young Queen has given her heart to the great Prime Minister of England, the Duke of Buckingham. And he loves her too."

"But how do you know all this?"

"From my wife," said the man. "She also told me that the Queen has been very frightened for several weeks now. She fears that

Monsieur Bonacieux's Secret

the Cardinal is trying to lure the Duke to Paris and trap him, just to disgrace her."

"But what does all this have to do with your wife's kidnapping?" asked D'Artagnan.

"The Queen confides all her secrets to my dear Constance, and I fear that the Cardinal is trying to learn those secrets."

"Do you know who actually kidnapped her?"

"I do not know his name, but I can describe him. He's a tall, dark nobleman with a black moustache, a scar on his right cheek, and a patch over his left eye."

"Why, that's my man of Meung!" cried D'Artagnan. "Are you sure of the description?"

"As sure as my name is Bonacieux!" said the man.

"Your name is Bonacieux? It seems that I have heard that name before."

"That is quite possible, Monsieur. I am

The Mysterious Kidnapper

your landlord. And since your very important duties have made you forget to pay your rent for three months, I thought you might find the time to help me and...."

"Of course, Monsieur Bonacieux!" cried D'Artagnan. "Just tell me the rest."

Bonacieux took a letter from his pocket. "I received this last night," he said.

D'Artagnan read: YOUR WIFE WILL BE RETURNED TO YOU WHEN SHE IS NO LONGER NEEDED. LOOK FOR HER AND YOU FACE ARREST!

"Oh, Monsieur!" cried Bonacieux. "I am terrified of being thrown into the Bastille. Please help me, and I shall forget about the three months rent."

"Yes," said D'Artagnan, "that is an excellent reason. You have won me over."

As soon as Bonacieux had left, D'Artagnan sent Planchet to find Athos, Porthos, and Aramis.

When the Three Musketeers arrived,

The Kidnapper's Letter

D'Artagnan told them of Monsieur Bonacieux's problem. Just as he was finishing the story, the landlord burst into the room crying, "Save me! They're here to arrest me!"

Four armed soldiers of the Cardinal's Guards stood at the door.

"Come in gentlemen!" called D'Artangnan. "We are all loyal to the King and to the Cardinal. If you have come for this man, then take him!"

"But you promised...." cried Bonacieux.

"We can only save you if we are free," whispered D'Artagnan. "If we are arrested, we cannot help you or your wife."

So Bonacieux let himself be led away by the Cardinal's Guards.

As soon as they were gone, Athos said, "You have acted wisely, D'Artagnan."

"Thank you, my friend. And now, gentlemen, from this moment on, we are at war with the Cardinal!"

The Cardinal's Guards Arrest Bonacieux.

D'Artagnan Spies on Bonacieux's Apartment.

Chapter 5
A Plot at the Court

After Bonacieux's arrest, the Cardinal's Guards kept a close watch on his first floor apartment. Whoever came there was stopped and questioned.

D'Artagnan was able to see and hear all that went on through a hole in the floor of his second-floor apartment. It was through this hole that he heard a woman's cries that night.

"The scoundrels!" he muttered. "They're tying her up and searching her!"

"But I tell you I live here!" the woman cried. "I am Madame Bonacieux."

"Madame Bonacieux!" murmured D'Artagnan. "Then she is now free...but what's that? They're dragging her away."

D'Artagnan sprang to his feet, grabbed his sword, and ran to the window.

"What are you going to do, Monsieur? cried Planchet.

"I am going down to try to stop them."

D'Artagnan grasped the windowsill and dropped to the ground. He kicked the front door open and rushed inside with his sword flying in front of him.

Several minutes later, four of the Cardinal's Guards came running out the door. Their uniforms were torn to ribbons.

Inside, D'Artagnan stood gazing at Madame Bonacieux, who had fainted in an armchair. She was a lovely young woman about twenty-five years old. "Much too young for that old husband of hers!" he thought. "But that's what comes from these arranged

D'Artagnan Springs into Action.

marriages!"

The woman seemed to be coming to her senses. "Ah, Monsieur," she said, stretching her arms out to D'Artangnan, "you saved me. But how did you know?"

"Your husband came to me for help in rescuing you," he replied.

"I escaped from the room where I was being held by lowering myself with sheets out the window," she explained.

"Clever girl!" said D'Artagnan, smiling. "We must talk some more, but it is not safe here. The guards will return soon."

"I must return to the palace tonight," she cried. "The Queen needs me urgently. Will you help me? You are young and brave, and my husband is old and cowardly. He would not help me if it meant danger for him."

"You can trust me, Constance," said D'Artagnan. "From the first minute I saw you, I knew I would do anything for you."

"You Saved Me."

"Oh, thank you," she whispered. "You will have my love and the Queen's gratitude if you help us."

"Just tell me how I may serve you," said D'Artagnan, kneeling at her feet.

"I fear that the Cardinal's Guards may be searching for me," she said. "Please follow me back to the palace to see that I get there safely."

"Do not fear, my sweet Constance. No harm shall come to you. I swear it!"

So Constance started out, and D'Artagnan kept about twenty paces behind her. After several minutes, she stopped at a doorway and knocked three times. The door opened and a shadowy figure came out to join her.

When the man placed his arm around Constance's shoulder, D'Artagnan flew into a rage. How could she betray him after pledging her love to him only minutes before?

D Artagnan jumped in front of them and

Why Has Constance Stopped?

blocked their way.

"What do you want, sir?" asked the man in a foreign accent. "Let us pass!"

"Take your hands off this lady!" cried D'Artagnan, grabbing Constance's arm.

"Oh, D'Artagnan," whispered Constance, "I asked you to follow me, not to interrupt me."

"Interrupt you? When you run into the arms of another man!" cried D'Artagnan, drawing his sword.

At the same moment, the man drew his.

"In the name of Heaven, Milord, stop!" cried Constance, throwing herself between the two men.

"Milord?" asked D'Artagnan. "Good Heavens, you must be..."

"Yes." said Constance, "it is the Duke of Buckingham. I am taking him to the Queen."

"A thousand pardons, Milord," said D'Artagnan, kneeling. "I love Madame Bonacieux, and I fear I let my jealousy put you in

"In the Name of Heaven, Milord, Stop!"

danger. How may I beg your forgiveness?"

"You are a brave young man," said the Duke. "You can best serve us by following us to the palace. Kill anyone who stops us!"

"Oh yes, Milord," said D'Artagnan. And he followed them to a side entrance of the palace until they disappeared through two heavy iron doors.

Constance led the Duke up a dark staircase and into a small candlelit room.

"Anne!" cried the Duke, falling to his knees in front of the Queen of France.

"Why have you come, Milord?" she whispered, her face frozen in fear. "You knew that the Cardinal was trying to trap you. You risk your life and my honor!"

"I had to see you. It was worth any risk!"

"But it is madness!" cried Anne. "The Cardinal is gathering proof to ruin me!"

"Dear, dear Anne," whispered the Duke, taking her in his arms.

"Why Have You Come, Milord?"

"Oh, Milord," she sobbed into his chest, "I am married to the King. I cannot disgrace him though I do not love him. Please go!"

"Yes, I will. But until I see you again, give me something to remember you by—a ring, a chain, anything I can wear to remind me of you."

Anne unfastened a ribbon from her neck. It was studded with twelve large diamonds. "Take this as a token of my love, Milord," she said, placing it in his hands.

The Duke of Buckingham gazed at the woman he loved. "The next time I return to you, Anne," he said, "I will not have to hide. For I will have conquered France!"

Buckingham lifted the Queen's hand to his lips, then rushed from the room.

Constance led him out of the palace and back to the house where he had been hiding. There, a coach was waiting to carry him to the coast and to England.

A Token of the Queen's Love

Monsieur Bonacieux Is Questioned.

Chapter 6
The Cardinal's Spies

Meanwhile, Monsieur Bonacieux had been arrested and taken to the Bastille. In an underground cell, he was questioned by an officer of the Cardinal's Guards.

"Prisoner," said the officer, "you and your wife are accused of plotting against France."

"Plotting? But I know nothing," cried Bonacieux. "And my wife has been kidnapped."

"Do you know who kidnapped her?"

"I suspect it was a tall, dark nobleman who wears a patch over his left eye."

The officer stopped writing and looked up

in surprise. "This is a matter for the Cardinal himself to handle," he said.

He summoned two guards who led Bonacieux out of the Bastille and into a closed carriage. The carriage sped across Paris and finally stopped at the back door of a large dark building. Bonacieux was pushed through the door and up a flight of stairs.

Inside an elegantly furnished room, he found himself facing a gray-haired man of medium height. The man had a proud face and piercing eyes. A small red cap covered the back of his head, and his long red robe hung to the floor. Around his neck, he wore a large gold cross. This man was Cardinal Richelieu—the most powerful man in France!

"So you are Bonacieux!" said the Cardinal with a sneer. "You are accused of plotting against France along with your wife and the Duke of Buckingham."

"But my wife has been kidnapped,

Cardinal Richelieu

Monseigneur! And when I described her kidnapper to your officer at the Bastille, he brought me here."

The Cardinal picked up a silver bell and rang it. Seconds later, a tall, dark man with a patch over his left eye appeared at the door.

"It is he!" cried Bonacieux. "The man who kidnapped my wife!"

Richelieu smiled and rang the bell again. Two guards entered. "Take this prisoner out," he ordered, "and hold him until I need him."

As soon as the door had closed behind Bonacieux, Richelieu turned to the man and smiled. "Well, Rochefort," he said, "you have been recognized by that idiot, Bonacieux. But no matter! What have you to report, my friend?"

"Hardly your friend, Eminence! Rather your most trusted spy. However, this time I failed you. I've let Madame Bonacieux escape. But she is no longer important, for I have far

Bonacieux Recognizes the Kidnapper.

more interesting news. The Queen and the Duke have seen each other at the palace."

"What took place between them?" asked Richelieu .

"One of the Queen's ladies-in-waiting was listening behind a curtain," said Rochefort, "and she reported that the Queen gave Buckingham her ribbon of diamond studs as a token of her love. That should be of great interest to King Louis, since he gave her those studs on her last birthday."

"Very well done, Rochefort!" said the Cardinal. "Those diamonds, which are now in England, shall be the Queen's downfall! I shall contact Milady de Winter in London. She is at the court quite often and is sure to see the Duke wearing the studs. I shall have her steal two studs and bring them to me."

Richelieu sat down and quickly wrote the letter. "Here," he said, handing it to Rochefort, "give it to your fastest horseman

Richelieu Plots the Queen's Downfall.

and tell him to leave for London immediately. And have the guards bring Bonacieux back in."

The terrified man entered and fell to his knees. "How can I convince Your Eminence of my innocence?" he cried.

"Rise, my friend," said Richelieu, offering his hand. "I have been mistaken about you. You are an honest man."

"The Cardinal believes me!" cried Bonacieux joyously. "He calls me his friend."

"Yes, my friend," replied Richelieu, his voice full of pretended sympathy. "You have been unjustly arrested, and I must apologize. Here, take this sack of one hundred pistoles, and do not be angry with me."

Bonacieux bowed to the ground. "Oh, thank you, Monseigneur! You are a great man!"

But the great man was thinking, "Ah, now I have another spy! One who shall spy on his wife!"

Richelieu Apologizes.

A Letter from Milady

Chapter 7
The Diamond Studs

Milady received Richelieu's letter, and two weeks later she sent the following reply:
I HAVE THE TWO DIAMOND STUDS, BUT I SHALL NEED MONEY TO GET TO PARIS. MILADY.
Richelieu figured out that it would take five days to send the money to England and another five days for Milady to return to Paris. That gave him ten days to start making his plans.

First, he called on the King. "Your Majesty," he began, "the Queen seems rather unhappy lately, and I thought perhaps a ball might please her. Then she could wear the twelve magnificent diamond studs you gave her on her birthday."

"Splendid idea!" exclaimed the King. "I shall inform Her Majesty of the ball immediately. When shall we have it?"

"Ten days from now will be fine, Sire."

"Fine! Fine! I shall tell Her Majesty to plan for a ball on October third."

"And do not forget to tell her how much you want to see her wearing the diamonds!"

King Louis hurried to the Queen's apartment and told her of the ball in her honor in ten days time. When he informed her that she was to wear the diamond studs, she gasped and turned pale.

Once the King had left, the Queen fell to her knees and buried her head in her hands. "I am lost!" she sobbed. "The Cardinal must know that I do not have the studs, and he plans to disgrace me at the ball."

"Perhaps I can help, Your Majesty," came a

"You Are to Wear Your Diamond Studs."

voice from behind a curtain.

"Oh, Constance, you heard? Is there anyone who can get the studs back from the Duke?"

"I will find a messenger I can trust," said Constance, "but he will need a letter in your hand for the Duke to believe him."

"Yes, yes," cried the Queen as she hurried to her desk. After she wrote the letter, she handed it to Constance along with a bag containing one thousand pistoles. "This will reward you and your messenger, my dear. If you succeed, you will have saved my honor!"

Constance returned home and burst in on her husband whom she hadn't seen for a week. "We must have a talk," she said. "You can do a good deed and make a great deal of money."

"A great deal of money?" said Bonacieux, wetting his lips at the thought.

"A thousand pistoles if you will deliver a letter to an important person in London."

A Letter for the Duke

"London? More plots! Nothing but plots!" he cried. "Plots can only put me back in the Bastille. I know all about these plots from the Cardinal. And I want no part of them!"

"The Cardinal? You have seen the Cardinal?"

"Yes! He called me his friend and gave me a hundred pistoles," said Bonacieux, proudly holding up the bag of gold coins. "So I will not allow you to get involved in plots against him or against France just for the sake of the Queen!"

Constance trembled as she realized how close she had come to betraying the Queen to this weak, greedy, cowardly man.

And Bonacieux realized that he had missed an opportunity to learn some information which might be useful to the Cardinal. So he decided to try to find out more about the trip.

"My dear Constance," he said sweetly, "since I love you so, I cannot refuse you. To

Bonacieux Wants No Part of Any Plots.

whom must I take that letter?"

"No, never mind!" she said, realizing the game her husband was playing. "It was not important, just about a woman's purchase."

Bonacieux decided that he had better report his information to the Cardinal anyway. He told his wife that he had an important business appointment, but he would return soon to escort her back to the palace.

As soon as the door shut behind him, Constance exploded. "You weren't bad enough before this," she shouted, "but now you're a spy for the Cardinal! I never loved you, you villain, but now I hate you! I swear you shall pay for this!"

No sooner had she uttered these words, than a knock on the ceiling made her raise her head.

A voice called down through a hole, "Come up the back way, my dear Constance. Perhaps I can help you."

"You Shall Pay for This!"

D'Artagnan Offers to Help Constance.

Chapter 8
A Mission to London

"You heard?" asked Constance as D'Artagnan opened the door for her.

"Yes," he replied. "The Queen needs a brave, loyal, intelligent man to go to London for her. So here I am!"

Constance's eyes, which had been blazing with hatred for her husband, now smiled at the brave young man. "Thank you, D'Artagnan. I know I can trust you," she said.

"I would rather die than have any harm come to you or the Queen!"

Constance took from her pocket the bag of pistoles her husband had shown her and handed it to D'Artagnan. "Here, you will need money for your trip," she said.

D'Artagnan burst out laughing. "The Cardinal's gold!" he cried. "I shall save the Queen with the Cardinal's money. How amusing!"

"Shh!" whispered Constance. "I hear voices below. I think it's my husband."

D'Artagnan and Constance put their heads close to the hole in the floor. Bonacieux and a man in a cloak were in the room below.

D'Artagnan gasped when he saw that the man was the nobleman who had stolen his letter in Meung.

"That is Count Rochefort," whispered Constance. "He's the man who kidnapped me."

"She is gone!" they heard Bonacieux cry. "But she's probably returned to the palace."

"Are you sure she didn't suspect you when you left?" asked Rochefort.

"No!" replied Bonacieux scornfully. "She is

Familiar Voices Below

too stupid for that."

"Oh, the beast!" hissed Constance.

"This time, you were the stupid one, Bonacieux," said Rochefort. "You should have taken the letter and brought it to...."

"I can still get it," interrupted Bonacieux. "My Constance adores me. She will give me the letter, and I will bring it right to the Cardinal."

"Oh, the traitor!" cried Constance after her husband and Rochefort had left. "But I have no time for anger now. I must get to the Queen and you must leave for England."

D'Artagnan kissed Constance good-bye and left the house. He would have to stop at Monsieur de Tréville's office to get a leave of absence from his company.

Tréville listened to D'Artagnan's request and then said, "You realize, do you not, that the Cardinal will try to stop you?"

"Yes, Monsieur, and that is why I'd like to

"You Were the Stupid One, Bonacieux."

take Athos, Porthos, and Aramis with me. That way, one of us is sure to get through."

"Good idea!" said Tréville as he handed D'Artagnan four passes.

Within the hour, four riders galloped out of Paris and rode north on the Calais Road.

Their trip went well until they stopped at an inn the following day. They were just finishing their meal when a drunk at the next table asked Porthos to drink a toast to the Cardinal.

"Certainly, my good man," said the Musketeer, "if you will then drink to the King."

"I will never drink to the King," cried the drunk, drawing his sword.

Porthos was never one to walk away from a fight, so he called to his friends to go on without him.

Hours later, the three riders approached a group of men who appeared to be repairing the road. Suddenly, the workmen picked up

A Drunk Seeks a Fight.

muskets they had hidden in the dirt and began firing.

"It's an ambush!" cried D'Artagnan. "Don't stop to return their fire. Ride on!"

But before they could escape, a shell hit Aramis in the shoulder. Still he rode on. After two hours though, he was so weakened from the loss of blood that he decided to seek help at a farmhouse along the road.

Athos and D'Artagnan continued on the journey alone. After twenty straight hours on the road, they stopped at an inn to rest.

The innkeeper demanded payment in advance, so Athos followed him into his office with the money. Suddenly, four armed men jumped out from behind the door.

"I've been captured !" shouted Athos. "Go on, D'Artagnan! Quickly!"

D'Artagnan didn't need to be told twice. He jumped on his horse and galloped off.

Late the next day, he reached the seaport

An Ambush on the Road

town of Calais where the steamer left for England. As he neared the dock, he saw a tall man talking to the ship's captain.

"I must get across the channel to England immediately," said the man.

"Only with a pass from the Cardinal," said the captain. "Those orders arrived today.'

"I have that pass here," said the man as he took out the paper.

The captain examined the pass, then handed it back to the man. "That's fine, sir!" he said. "We don't sail for another hour, so you might be more comfortable waiting as the inn down the road."

As the man left the dock and came toward him, D'Artagnan saw the black patch. It was Count Rochefort!

D'Artagnan drew his sword and jumped in front of him. "Hand over that pass!" he cried.

"You!" cried Rochefort. "The Gascon rascal with the yellow horse! Where are your

A Pass to Cross the Channel

Musketeer friends to defend you now?"

"I need no one to defend me!" cried D'Artagnan, waving his sword. "I'll take that pass from your hand or from your dead body!"

Rochefort drew his sword, and the two men lunged at each other. Within minutes, D'Artagnan had wounded Rochefort three times, crying at each thrust, "One for Athos! One for Porthos! One for Aramis!"

Rochefort fell with the third thrust. Believing him to be dead, D'Artagnan reached down to search for the pass. But Rochefort was only wounded, and he plunged his sword into D'Artagnan's chest, crying, "One for you!"

"And one for me!" cried D'Artagnan, running his sword through Rochefort's shoulder.

D'Artagnan found the pass and hurried to the ship. On board, he examined his wound and found that it was not serious. But he was exhausted from his long journey, so he

"One for Me!"

stretched out on the deck and went to sleep. The next morning, the ship docked in Dover, and D'Artagnan set foot for the first time on English soil.

While he was waiting for a hired horse to be saddled, he looked around at the passengers waiting to cross to France. A beautiful blonde woman caught his eye. It was the woman in the carriage at Meung, the one called Milady! Was she the reason Rochefort was going to England? No matter! D'Artagnan had to get to London and get then quickly.

The door to the Duke of Buckingham's mansion was opened by his valet. "Who is calling, sir?" he asked.

"Just say the young man who challenge him to a duel in Paris," said D'Artagnan.

Buckingham came out immediately, his face white with fear. "Has something happened to the Queen?" he cried.

D'Artagnan Spies Milady in the Crowd.

"No, Milord. But she is in great danger, which she explains in this letter."

Buckingham took the letter. "Good Heavens!" he exclaimed. "What am I reading? Oh, my poor dear Anne! Quickly, my boy, follow me!"

Buckingham led D'Artagnan up the stairs and unlocked a door with a small gold key hanging from his neck. D'Artagnan followed the Duke into a candlelit chapel. A portrait of Queen Anne hung on the wall above an altar.

The Duke approached the altar and opened a small carved box. "Here," he said, lifting a ribbon of diamonds from the box. "Here are the precious diamond studs."

Suddenly he uttered a dreadful cry!

"What's the matter?" asked D'Artagnan.

"Two studs are missing!" exclaimed Buckingham. "Only ten are here!"

"Could you have lost them, Milord?"

Two of the Diamond Studs Are Missing!

"No, they have been stolen. See, the ribbon has been cut. Now who could...Wait! The only time I wore them was at court last week. Milady de Winter spent most of the evening with me. That's it! She must have stolen them for the Cardinal."

"I saw her boarding the steamer for France just hours ago," said D'Artagnan.

Then we must hurry," said the Duke as he rushed out of the chapel and called for D'Artagnan to follow him.

They ran through several corridors until they entered the workroom of the court jewelers.

"Look at these diamonds," said the Duke to the head jeweler, "and tell me how much each one is worth."

The jeweler examined them carefully, then replied, "Fifteen hundred pistoles each, Milord."

"And how many days would it take to make

"Tell Me How Much Each One Is Worth."

two studs exactly like them?" he asked.

"A week, at least, Milord."

"But that will be too late!" cried D'Artagnan. The ball is just five days off."

"I will give you three thousand pistoles each if you can make up two for me by tomorrow," said the Duke.

"My Lord," said the jeweler, "you shall have them."

True to his word, the jeweler presented the two diamonds to the Duke the following afternoon. They were so perfectly matched to the other ten that even Buckingham could not tell the difference.

"I have done all I can," said the Duke as he handed the diamonds to D'Artagnan. "The rest is up to you. I have a ship waiting to take you to France and horses for you when you arrive. We may meet soon as enemies on the field of battle, but today we part as friends, D'Artagnan. And I thank you!"

Twelve Perfectly Matched Diamonds

D'Artagnan **Receives Good News.**

Chapter 9
The Ball

D'Artagnan reached Paris on the evening of the ball. He stopped first at Monsieur de Tréville's to see if there was any news of his three friends.

"Yes," said Tréville, "they have returned and are recovering from their wounds."

Next, D'Artagnan went to the palace to rejoin his company on duty there and to give a special parcel to a great lady.

As the guests were gathering in the ballroom below, Cardinal Richelieu and King Louis were approaching the Queen's apartment to escort her down. As her doors opened and the Queen appeared, Richelieu whispered some words to the King. Louis looked at his wife's bare neck and demanded in a threatening voice, "Madame, why are you not wearing your diamond studs? You knew I specifically asked you to."

The Queen looked at the mocking smile on the Cardinal's face and replied to her husband, "Sire, in this great crowd, I feared that I would lose them."

"Well, you were wrong, Madame. I am highly displeased with you."

"Sire," said the Queen sweetly, "I can return to my rooms and put them on."

"Then do so, Madame! I shall await you downstairs. The ball is about to begin."

The Queen bowed and returned to her apartment with her ladies.

As Richelieu and the King slowly descended the staircase, the Cardinal placed a small box in the King's hands. The King opened

No Diamonds!

it and found two diamond studs.

"What does this mean?" he asked.

"Nothing," replied the Cardinal, "if the Queen has the diamond studs. If she does, which I very much doubt, then count them, Sire. And if there are only ten, not twelve, ask her what could have possibly happened to the other two—which you now hold in that box."

But before the King could question the Cardinal any further, a cry of admiration rose from the ballroom. All eyes were fixed on the beautiful woman at the top of the stairs—the Queen of France.

As she slowly and gracefully made her way down, two pairs of eyes gazed at the diamonds on her neck. The King gazed with joy, and the Cardinal, with annoyance. But she was still too far away for either man to count the studs.

As she approached, the King took her

Richelieu Sets a Trap.

hand, kissed it, and spoke. "I thank you Madame, for bowing to my wishes. But I think that two of your diamonds are missing, and I have brought them back to you."

"Oh, Sire," exclaimed the Queen, pretending surprise at the box he placed in her hands, "you are giving me two more. How kind of you! Now I shall have fourteen."

The King counted the studs on his wife's neck. There were twelve. He called the Cardinal to him. "What does this mean?" he demanded.

"This means, Sire, that I wished to present those two studs to Her Majesty. But I did not dare offer them myself, so I chose to give them to her through you."

The Queen's smile showed Richelieu that she was not fooled by his weak excuse. "Oh, Your Eminence," she said sweetly, "I am most grateful. Surely these two studs cost you as much as the other twelve cost His

The Queen Now Has Fourteen Studs.

Majesty."

Then she bowed to the King and descended into the ballroom to join her guests.

As she made her way through the crowd, she stopped in front of a young cadet on guard in the ballroom. She smiled and offered her hand to him. The cadet fell to his knees and pressed the royal hand respectfully to his lips. As the Queen withdrew her hand, she left a ring in the young man's hand. This, then, was D'Artagnan's reward for saving the Queen's honor!

Two of the guests watched the Queen and D'Artagnan with great interest—Cardinal Richelieu and Milady de Winter.

"So, the young Gascon arrived in time," said Milady. "What do you plan to do with this boy who has outwitted you? Will you plan some revenge on him?"

"Revenge?" said the Cardinal. "Hardly! I could use such a brave man on my side.

D'Artagnan's Reward

Perhaps I will try to win him over."

"Your Eminence loses gracefully, but I do not. I failed in my mission because of him and that woman he loves. I shall have my revenge on both of them."

"That woman? Oh yes, Madame Bonacieux," said the Cardinal. "She must be stopped from carrying those letters between the Queen and the Duke, and from arranging their meetings. Send Rochefort to me immediately!"

"Yes, Your Eminence," replied Milady with a smile. She would have her revenge!

Rochefort was still weak from the wounds he had received from D'Artagnan's sword at Calais. But when the Cardinal gave him orders to imprison Madame Bonacieux, he, too, saw it as a way to take his revenge on D'Artagnan. His revenge was for the wounds D'Artagnan had inflicted and for the disgrace of having been robbed of his pass to England. Yes, the Gascon would pay dearly!

Plans for Revenge

D'Artagnan Sees an Attack.

Chapter 10
Milady de Winter

D'Artagnan remained at his post until the ball was over at four o'clock in the morning. When his company was dismissed in the square outside the palace, D'Artagnan hurried to meet Constance. Earlier, when he had given her the diamonds she had promised to meet him after the ball.

He was no more than ten paces into a side street when he spied a carriage ahead of him. A beautiful blonde young woman was leaning out the window, fighting off an attacker who seemed to be pulling her out.

"Villain!" cried D'Artagnan as he rushed

towards the carriage with his sword drawn.

The woman looked up at the young cadet and whispered to her attacker, "Run quickly! You have played your part well."

The man jumped down from the step of the carriage and headed into a dark alley. D'Artagnan chased him, but the man had disappeared. He returned breathlessly to the carriage.

"Are you hurt, Madame?" he asked, gazing at the woman's exquisite beauty.

"No, Monsieur," said Milady de Winter, "but I thank you for coming to my rescue. You are a brave young man and I am most grateful. How may I reward you?"

"I am rewarded by seeing that you are safe," said D'Artagnan, who could not tear his eyes away from the woman's face.

"Then you must call on me tomorrow, so that I might thank you again," she said. "Here is my name and my address."

D'Artagnan Gazes at Milady's Beauty.

D'Artagnan took the paper with trembling hands. "Th-thank you, Milady," he stammered, "I would be honored to call."

With that, the coachman whipped the horses, and the carriage sped off into the darkness.

"This will be so easy," muttered Milady with a smile. "It will be child's play."

"I am the happiest of men!" shouted D'Artagnan as he ran through the streets. "My heart is bursting with love, not once, but twice!"

When he arrived back at his apartment, Constance was not there. D'Artagnan paced the floors for hours, watching the sun rise over Paris. When he could stand it no more. he decided to talk to Athos. Surely the Musketeer knew everything when it came to women.

"Never trust a woman—any woman!" exclaimed Athos when D'Artagnan finished

Waiting for Constance

telling him of Constance's broken promise.

"But she seemed to love me so dearly," said D'Artagnan, "and I love her. How could she have used me for this mission and then just leave me? Have you ever loved, Athos?"

"Love! Bah!" cried Athos. "Let me tell you a story of what love did to someone—to one of my friends, not me, of course. He was a nobleman—one of the counts of my province—a rich, kind-hearted, handsome nobleman who could have married any woman he chose.

"But he fell in love with a girl of sixteen, as blonde and as beautiful as any woman he had ever seen. My friend knew nothing about her, only that she had come to live in the province with her brother, a priest. My friend was an honorable man, and although he could have taken her as his mistress, he chose, instead, to marry her.

"He gave her his name, his wealth, and his

"Love! Bah!"

love. But he was a fool and an idiot!"

"But why, if he loved her?" asked D'Artagnan.

"Because one day, shortly after they were married, he discovered a horrible secret about her. She had fallen from her horse while they were riding. Her sleeve slipped from the neck of her dress and bared her shoulder. And there, he discovered a brand. The brand of the *fleur-de-lis*! The brand of a thief who has stolen sacred treasures from the church."

"And what did the count do?"

"The only thing he could do. The law stated that such a crime had to be punished by death. So he hung her from a tree!"

Athos buried his face in his hands and sobbed. "That cured me of beautiful, blonde, loving women," he added, forgetting to end his story by referring to "the count."

"Then she is dead?" asked D'Artagnan.

"I imagine so," said Athos as he uncorked

The Brand of the *Fleur-de-Lis*!

a bottle of wine and poured two drinks.

"And her brother, the priest?"

"I went after him the next day, but he had disappeared," replied Athos, sighing.

The two friends proceeded to empty that bottle of wine, then three or four more. As evening approached, D'Artagnan realized that he was expected at Milady de Winter's home at eight. He told Athos of his meeting with her the night before, but Athos seemed surprised.

"Isn't this the woman you believe to be a spy for the Cardinal?" he asked.

"Yes, my friend," said D'Artagnan, "yet I still feel this great attraction to her."

"Ah, D'Artagnan, you have just told me how you lost the woman you love. And now you are running after this Milady de Winter without any thought of your dear Constance. Well, enjoy yourself, my friend, but beware of a trap at all times!"

Athos' Advice about Women

And so began D'Artagnan's visits to the beautiful Milady de Winter. Day after day he called upon her, falling more and more in love with her at each visit and thinking less and less of the original suspicions he had had about her.

After a month had gone by, D'Artagnan called one day and was surprised to learn that Milady wasn't in. Her maid, a pretty young girl named Kitty, led D'Artagnan into the house just the same.

"Monsieur," she said, "I must speak to you in private."

"Of course! What is it, Kitty?"

"You love my mistress very much, don't you, sir?" she asked fearfully.

"Oh, more than I can tell you!"

"That is a great pity, sir, for my mistress does not love you at all. She is using you for her own purposes."

D'Artagnan was shocked. "Why are you

Milady Isn't In.

telling me all this?" he demanded.

"Because, Monsieur, in love it is every woman for herself," she admitted boldly.

Then D'Artagnan remembered the loving glances Kitty had given him each time he entered the house. If what she said about Milady was, true, then Kitty just might be useful to him. He reached out to embrace her. Just then, they heard the front door slam.

"Good Heavens!" cried Kitty. "My mistress has returned. You must leave quickly!"

D'Artagnan picked up his hat as if to go, but seeing that Kitty had already left the room, he hid himself in the maid's closet.

"I'm coming, Milady," he heard her call.

The two women went into Milady's bedroom, but the door had been left open. He could hear them talking.

"Well, Kitty," said Milady, "has my young Gascon called on me this evening?"

"No, Madame," lied the maid. "Can the

D'Artagnan Hides in Kitty's Closet.

young man have found another love?"

"Hardly, my dear," said Milady. "He is too much in love with me. I have a good enough hold on him."

"But I thought that Milady loved him."

"Love him? I detest him! He is an idiot! He made me fail in my mission for the Cardinal. But I shall have my revenge on him!"

D'Artagnan shuddered to hear the woman he loved speak of him this way.

"I have been planning my revenge against him for several weeks now," continued Milady .

"But Madame already has had her revenge against the woman he was in love with," said Kitty.

"Oh, that Bonacieux woman! He has forgotten that she ever existed. I saw to that. With the help of Count Rochefort, I have taken care of her!"

A cold sweat broke out on D'Artagnan's

Milady Has Plans for Revenge.

brow. This woman was a monster! He had to find out what she had done with Constance.

He rushed from the closet and burst into Milady's room. "You have betrayed me, you miserable woman!" he cried.

Milady turned pale and backed away from him. She reached inside her dress and pulled out a knife. Her face twisted with rage, she sprang at D'Artagnan. He quickly grabbed her wrist and forced the knife from her clenched hand. She fell to her knees and D'Artagnan's hands tightened around her throat.

"Where is Constance Bonacieux?" he cried. "Tell me where she is or I shall squeeze the life out of you!"

Milady pulled violently at a heavy brooch pinned to her dress. Once it was free, she dug its point into D'Artagnan's face just below his eye.

D'Artagnan loosened his hold on her throat

"Where Is Constance Bonacieux?"

for an instant and grabbed the brooch out of her hand. But in that instant, she broke free and rushed to a table for another dagger.

As she came at him in a fury, D'Artagnan drew his sword and backed towards the door. She lunged with the dagger, and D'Artagnan's sword caught the sleeve of her dress, splitting it in two at the top.

To his great astonishment, that lovely white shoulder bore the brand of the *fleur-de-lis*, the brand of the public executioner!

"Good God!" cried D'Artagnan, frozen in his tracks at the door.

"Villain!" cried Milady. "You now know my terrible secret, but you shall never live to reveal it!"

As she raised the dagger above his heart, D'Artagnan recovered his senses. He turned and fled out the door, bolting it after him.

He raced down the stairs and out into the street with Milady's screams following him.

A *Fleur-de-Lis!*

He didn't stop running until he burst into Athos' front door.

"Something terrible has happened to me!" he cried breathlessly.

"Does it have something to do with that brooch you are clutching in your hand?" asked Athos.

D'Artagnan looked down. He hadn't realized that the brooch he had grabbed from Milady was still clutched in his fist. He nodded.

"Let me look at it," said Athos, taking it from D'Artagnan. He turned the brooch over in his hand and examined it carefully. Suddenly, he turned pale. "It is difficult to believe that there could be two like this in the whole world," he whispered.

"Do you recognize it?" asked D'Artagnan.

"Yes! It was in my family for generations before I gave it to her. . .to my wife! But tell me, how did you get the brooch?"

Milady's Brooch

D'Artagnan explained all that had happened in Milady's apartment. When he came to the part where he had discovered the *fleur-de-lis* on her shoulder, Athos groaned and turned pale. His head fell between his hands.

"This woman, this Milady, is she blonde?"

"Yes," replied D'Artagnan.

"Are her eyes the lightest blue?"

"Yes."

"Is she tall and well-built?"

"Yes."

"And the *fleur-de-lis*, is it small and red?"

"Yes."

"Yet you say she is English?"

"They call her Milady, an English name, but she could be French. She speaks perfectly, with no trace of a foreign accent."

"Then the worst of my fears has come true," cried Athos. "Oh, God! I had hoped that she was dead! But she has returned to

Athos' Terrible Discovery

haunt me."

"You mean...that woman...the one in your province...the one who was branded...."

"Yes, D'Artagnan. That woman and Milady de Winter are the same. She is my...my wife! And now that you know her secret, she will never let you live. You must leave France. You must get away immediately!"

"But what about you, Athos?"

"I shall be safe enough. She doesn't know that Athos exists. She doesn't know that the Count de la Fère became the Musketeer, Athos. But she does know about you, and she will be after you."

"My company leaves for La Rochelle tomorrow to fight the Huguenots," said D'Artagnan. "That should keep me far enough away from her for a while."

"You can never be far enough away from that woman, my boy. Take my warning!"

"She Will Never Let You Live."

La Rochelle

Chapter 11
Plans for Revenge

For many years, the French Catholics and the French Protestants, the Huguenots, lived in peace together. The Huguenots held several towns and ruled themselves without interference from the Catholic King, Louis XIII.

Then Richelieu decided to unite all of France under his Catholic rule, and his armies quickly overpowered all of the Huguenot towns except La Rochelle. The battle for La Rochelle had been going on for fifteen months when the Cardinal and the King arrived with their guards and their

Musketeers.

One evening, when the King's Musketeers were off duty, Athos, Porthos, and Aramis obtained a pass to go into a nearby town. D'Artagnan's company of guards was on duty in the trenches, so he couldn't join them.

After several hours of drinking at the Red Dove Inn, the Three Musketeers started back to camp. At a turn in the road, they saw two riders coming towards them.

"Who goes there?" called Athos in a firm voice. His hand was on his pistol.

"Who are you?" said one of the horsemen in an even firmer voice.

Athos realized that it might be one of the officers making his night rounds, so he replied, The King's Musketeers."

The riders stopped a few feet away. Their long cloaks hid their faces. The same commanding voice said, "Your names, gentlemen?"

The Musketeers Meet Two Riders.

Athos was becoming annoyed. "Who are you, sir," he demanded, "and what right do you have to question us?"

The officer let his cloak fall, leaving his face uncovered.

"The Cardinal!" cried the Musketeers.

"Ah! I see now who you gentlemen are," said Richelieu, "Monsieur Athos, Monsieur Porthos, and Monsieur Aramis. I know that you are not exactly my friends, but I also know that you are all brave men. Therefore, I shall ask ycu to accompany me to the Red Dove Inn."

"We shall be honored, Your Eminence," said Athos. "Besides, we passed some suspicious-looking men on the road and even had a quarrel with one at the inn."

"A quarrel, gentlemen?" said the Cardinal. "You know I don't approve of quarrels."

"But, Your Eminence, the man was drunk,

"The Cardinal!"

and he was trying to break down the door of a lady who had arrived earlier."

"Was this lady young and blonde and beautiful?" asked the Cardinal anxiously.

"We did not see her," said Athos.

"Ah! You did not see her," said the Cardinal with a sigh of relief. "Well, you did right in defending her. Now, let us be off!"

When they arrived at the inn, the innkeeper came running out, bowing to the Cardinal.

Richelieu asked, "Have you a room on the ground floor where these gentlemen can warm themselves while they wait for me?"

The innkeeper nodded and led the Musketeers into a large room. The Cardinal hurried up the stairs as if he knew the place well.

Porthos and Aramis sat before the fire and amused themselves with a game of dice. Athos, meanwhile, paced back and forth,

Waiting for the Cardinal

wondering who the Cardinal was meeting here. As he passed in front of an old stovepipe which ran up through the ceiling and into the room above, Athos heard the murmur of voices. The words coming down through the pipe caught his attention, and he made a sign for his friends to be silent. He put his ear close to the pipe and heard the Cardinal talking.

"Listen, Milady! Here are your orders. You are to leave for England tonight to meet with the Duke of Buckingham."

"But I fear that the Duke will not trust me, not after the affair of the diamond studs," said a woman's voice that made Athos gasp.

"I am not sending you to gain his trust," said Richelieu. "You will simply deliver this message. If he carries out his plans to send English forces to help the Huguenots, it will mean not only war with France, but ruin for the Queen as well."

Athos Hears Voices from Upstairs.

"What if he doesn't believe me?"

"Just assure him that I have proof which will disgrace the Queen."

"And if he still insists on going ahead with his plans?"

"Then the Duke must meet with. . .an accident!"

"I shall see to that gladly!" said MiJady. "And then I shall take care of nay own enemies. First, that woman Bonacieux. . . . "

"But she is in the prison at Nantes."

"Not any longer. Your Eminence. The Queen found out where she was and had her taken to a convent for safety."

"Which convent?" asked the Cardinal.

"It's is being kept a secret," said Milady.

"Well, I shall find out and let you know."

"Good! And now for my other enemy," continued Milady, "the man who made my mission with the diamonds a failure, the man who wounded Rochefort, and the man who

Richelieu Gives Milady Her Orders.

tried to kill me when he learned that I was involved in the kidnapping of his Constance."

"You mean D'Artagnan," said the Cardinal. "I can easily send him to the Bastille, where he will never be heard from again."

"Your Eminence," said Milady, "that's a fair exchange. The life of D'Artagnan for the life of Buckingham! Now, I shall need a signed warrant giving me the authority to do anything I need to... for the good of France, of course."

Richelieu sat down at a table, and Athos heard the scratching of a pen. Athos turned away from the stovepipe and led Porthos and Aramis to the far end of the room.

"I must leave you for a while," he said.

"But what shall we tell the Cardinal?" asked Porthos.

"Simply tell him that I have gone on ahead to make sure the road is safe. Once you both reach camp, stay at D'Artagnan's side. Do not

Richelieu Writes Out the Warrant.

leave him for an instant!"

Athos then rushed from the room and galloped off toward La Rochelle.

Minutes later, Richelieu came down, ready to return to camp. Porthos explained Athos' absence, but assured the Cardinal that he and Aramis were ready to escort His Eminence back to La Rochelle.

Meanwhile, as soon as Athos was out of sight of the inn, he stopped his horse behind a large rock. He waited there until he saw his friends and the Cardinal pass by. Then he turned around and sped back to the inn.

He explained to the innkeeper that the Cardinal had forgotten to tell the lady something of importance and that he had returned with the message.

"Go on up," said the innkeeper. "She is still in her room."

Athos hurried up the stairs. Through the open door, he saw Milady putting on her hat.

Athos Watches the Cardinal Pass By.

He entered the room and closed the door behind him softly. As he turned the lock, Milady spun around.

"Who are you?' she cried. "How dare you enter my room!"

Athos raised his hat and pulled his cloak away from his face. "Do you not recognize me, Madam?" he asked.

Milady gasped! The Count de la Fère," she cried, turning pale and backing away.

"Yes, Milady, the Count de la Fère! You believed I was dead, didn't you? Just as I believed you to be dead too."

Milady groaned.

But Athos went on. "The Count de la Fère has been hidden for years behind the name of the Musketeer, Athos, just as Charlotte de Beuil has been hidden behind the name of Milady de Winter. But neither Charlotte de Beuil nor Milady de Winter can hide the brand of the *fleur-de-lis* from her body!"

Milady Recognizes the Count de la Fère.

"Wh-what do you want with me?" stammered Milady in a trembling, terrified voice.

"Hear what I have to say, Madame," said Athos coldly. "I don't much care what you do with the Duke of Buckingham. He is an Englishman and so, my enemy. But if you dare touch a single hair on D'Artagnan's head, I swear I'll kill you with my bare hands. And this time, I'll make sure you're dead!"

Milady stood frozen with fear.

"And now, Madame," continued Athos, raising his pistol to Milady's head, "give me the warrant the Cardinal just signed. You have five seconds to do so. One... two...three...four...."

Just as his finger was about to squeeze the trigger, Milady reached into her dress and pulled out the paper.

"Take it!" she cried, throwing it at him. "I'll have my revenge on you too!"

Athos unfolded the paper and read, "IT IS BY

Athos Demands the Warrant.

MY ORDER AND FOR THE GOOD OF FRANCE THAT THE BEARER OF THIS LETTER HAS DONE WHAT HE HAS DONE. 3 DECEMBER 1627. RICHELIEU.

The Cardinal may have thought he was clever in giving you this permission to murder, Madame, but one day, this warrant will return to haunt him!"

Then Athos turned and left the room without once looking behind him. At the front door of the inn, he found the two men who were to escort Milady to her ship.

"Gentlemen," he said, "the Cardinal has asked me to remind you that you are to see that this woman gets to her ship. No one is to speak to her and she is to send no messages."

The men nodded and Athos rode off.

When he reached the camp at La Rochelle, he found Porthos and Aramis with D'Artagnan, who had just come off duty. The Three Musketeers told D'Artagnan what they had learned of Milady's plans.

A Permission to Murder!

"Good Heavens!" cried D'Artagnan. "We must warn the Queen, and she must warn the Duke. We cannot permit that evil woman to carry out her murderous plans."

"But we cannot leave our posts in the middle of battle," said Athos, "not even to save Buckingham ."

"But we can send my trusted Planchet," suggested D'Artagnan.

So they summoned Planchet from his tent and gave him a sealed letter for the Queen.

"You must ride to Paris immediately," said D'Artagnan, "then carry the Queen's message to London. But hurry! And ask her where my dear Constance has been taken."

"And now, my friends," said Porthos, "let us drink a toast to Planchet's success!"

"Splendid idea!" said D'Artagnan as he took out a bottle of wine and began pouring it for his friends. "And let me thank you for sending this wine, my friends. It was kind of

Pouring a Toast to Planchet's Success

you to think of me in the trenches while you were at the Red Dove Inn."

"We sent you no wine," said Athos.

"But this note from the innkeeper said it was from the three of you."

"What does it matter where the wine came from," said Porthos, lifting his glass. "Let us drink it just the same."

"No!" cried D'Artagnan, knocking the glass from his hand and rushing out of the tent. On the ground outside lay one of the guards from his company. The man was having terrible convulsions and choking. Then his body stiffened. He was dead from the wine D'Artagnan had poured for him moments before.

"Poisoned wine from the Red Dove Inn!" said Athos. "We can guess who sent it."

"We must prevent her from carrying out any more of her murderous plans," said D'Artagnan. "For she will never rest until all of us are dead!"

D'Artagnan Suspects the Wine.

Milady Arrives at Buckingham's Mansion.

Chapter 12
Milady's Murderous Deeds

As Planchet entered the gates of Paris two days later, Milady's carriage drew up to the gates of Buckingham's mansion. The Duke himself came out to greet her.

"I am here, Milord, as the messenger of Cardinal Richelieu," she said.

"Well, well, so the Cardinal's spy has returned," said Buckingham. "I regret that I have no more diamond studs for you to steal."

"I'm here to warn you that if you send ships and supplies to La Rochelle, His Eminence will ruin Her Majesty."

"You may inform His Eminence that I

shall not he persuaded either by his threats or by his spy's beauty. My ships shall leave for La Rochelle as planned."

"You will regret those words, My Lord Buckingham," cried Milady as she pulled a small revolver out of her purse.

In an instant, four guards grabbed her and pinned her arms behind her back.

"I shall tell His Eminence that you will not change your mind," she said.

"You shall tell His Eminence nothing!" cried the Duke. "I'm having you locked up in the Tower of London, which is as nice a place as his Bastille"

"You wouldn't dare!" she cried.

"No? Lieutenant Felton, come forward!" he called.

A young officer stepped forward and bowed to the Duke.

"Look at this woman, John," said Buckingham. "She is young and beautiful, but she is

Milady Attempts Murder.

a monster. I am placing her in your care at the Tower because I know of your loyalty to me. I have saved your life on the field of battle and promoted you up through the ranks in my service. I have treated you as I would my own son. This woman has come to England to kill me. So be on your guard! She might try to kill you too!"

"My Lord," said Felton, "your wishes shall be obeyed on my honor and on my life."

John Felton could not have known at that moment how Milady could use a man's honor or his life for her own purposes. And her purposes now were freedom and revenge. She was determined to use the young jailer for both.

She spent the first day and night in her cell on her knees in prayer, bursting into deep sobs when she heard Felton's footsteps approach. He was beginning to respect her as a religious person like he was.

Milady Carries Out Her Plan.

Then for days, she refused all food, begging her jailer to let her die. Or better still, to give her a knife to end her life more quickly. He was beginning to pity her.

At last, when she was convinced that Felton's respect and pity had turned to love, she threw herself at his feet crying, "Help me! Deliver me from my enemy!"

"Who is your enemy?" he asked, gently lifting her to her feet and holding her.

"The man who stole me away from my family when I was a pure young girl...the man who shamed me...the man you serve so loyally," she lied, with tears running down her face.

"Oh, Milady, surely you cannot mean the Duke of Buckingham!" cried Felton.

"It is he! It is he! Please let me die of this shame," she sobbed, throwing her arms around the young man's neck.

"No, no!" he said. "You shall not die. You

186

"Help me!"

shall live to have your revenge. And I shall help. Trust me, please, for I love you. I must leave now so that I can arrange for your escape, my dear lady.

As the door to the cell closed behind Felton, Milady smiled. Felton was hers!

When he returned two hours later, he led her quietly down the stone steps behind the prison. A small boat was tied up in the river below. They climbed in and Felton picked up the oars, pointing to a large sloop anchored near the mouth of the river. "I have hired that sloop to carry you back to France," he said. "You will be safe."

"But what about Buckingham?" she cried. "Do not let his evil deeds go unpunished!"

"Buckingham is preparing to set sail for La Rochelle," said Felton.

"He must not leave England!" she cried.

"Do not fear, my angel," whispered Felton. kissing her hand. "He shall not leave."

A Way Back to France

Milady smiled a victorious smile. She gazed into the face of the young man seated next to her. The death of the Duke of Buckingham was written all over that face!

Felton helped Milady aboard the sloop. He would return to shore, but he promised to be back on board by ten o'clock to make the voyage to France with her. He had three hours to avenge this beautiful woman who had sworn her love to him.

He headed towards the port, making his way through the troops marching towards the ships and through the crowds gathered to see them off. He felt for the knife hidden inside his jacket.

At that moment, he was jostled by a rather plump young man dressed in the clothing of a French lackey. "Pardon, Monsieur!" said the man in French, but Felton didn't bother answering Planchet's apologies; he just clutched his knife a little more tightly.

Felton's Murderous Mission

The Three Musketeers

Both men seemed to be rushing through the crowds in the direction of the Duke's ship. Felton could see Buckingham ahead, proudly displaying his fleet to the ministers of King Charles.

Planchet saw him too and began to run.

Suddenly, Felton burst through the line of noblemen. He leaped on the Duke and plunged the knife into his heart, crying, "Milady has been avenged!"

As the guards surrounded Felton and pinned him to the ground, Planchet stopped and stared in horror. He was a moment too late. The Duke of Buckingham was dead! Murdered!

The crowd was in an uproar as Felton was dragged away. A nearby clock struck eight, and Felton turned his gaze to the harbor. The sail of a sloop could be seen steering for the coast of France. The woman for whom he was sacrificing his life had not waited!

"Milady Has Been Avenged!"

Rochefort Arrives at the Inn.

Chapter 13
Murder Follows Murder

The moment Milady reached the coast of France, she sent off a message to Richelieu at La Rochelle. It read: I HAVE SUCCEEDED. BUCKINGHAM WILL NEVER LEAVE ENGLAND AGAIN. I AWAIT YOUR NEXT ORDERS. MILADY. The following day, a carriage pulled up in front of the inn where Milady had spent the night. A tall, dark nobleman got out.

The man was shown to Milady's room and he greeted her with a smile. "Your message arrived at La Rochelle a few hours ago," said Count Rochefort. "His Eminence was most pleased with your success."

"Good!" said Milady. "And now that the Cardinal's business is done, I shall devote myself to my own plans. Has His Eminence discovered where Madame Bonacieux is?"

"Of course, Milady," said Rochefort. "His Eminence always finds out what he wishes to know. She is at the convent in Bethune."

"Then we must prepare to leave immediately for Bethune," said Milady.

They went down the stairs and into Rochefort's waiting carriage. The Count called to the coachman to head for the convent at Bethune, and they started off.

Neither the Count nor Milady noticed the plump young man walking towards the inn from the ship that had just arrived from France. Neither did they realize that Planchet had recognized them and had heard Rochefort call out their destination.

"Bethune!" he muttered. "Why, that is where the Queen said Madame Bonacieux is

Planchet Overhears Their Destination.

hidden. I must warn my master."

Planchet hired a horse and rode at top speed to La Rochelle. In two hours, he burst into D'Artagnan's tent, panting.

"Welcome, Planchet!" cried D'Artagnan. "You arrive at our moment of victory. La Rochelle has fallen! But what news do you bring?"

"I fear, sire, that all is lost! The Duke has been murdered."

"Murdered!" cried D'Artagnan. "My God, that evil woman again! But that is done. What news do you have of Constance?

"She is at the convent at Bethune, sire. But others are already on their way there."

"Others? Which others?"

"Milady and Rochefort," explained Planchet as he told his master what he had heard at the inn.

"Oh no!" cried D'Artagnan. "My two deadliest enemies are about to murder my love!

Planchet Rushes to Warn D'Artagnan.

I must leave for Bethune immediately. Quickly, Planchet, summon Athos, Porthos, and Aramis while I arrange for a leave."

Meanwhile, the carriage bearing Milady and Rochefort entered the courtyard of the convent.

"Wait for me here," said Milady. "This vengeance shall be mine alone!"

Milady got out of the carriage and presented herself to the Mother Superior at the door of the convent.

"I am here on orders of His Eminence, the Cardinal," said Milady.

"Come in, my child," answered the nun. "How might we welcome you?"

"I have brought a message from His Eminence for Madame Bonacieux," said Milady.

"Oh, poor Constance has been so lonely all these months! How she will welcome you! Her room is just at the top of the stairs. You will find her at her prayers."

Milady Lies Her Way into the Convent.

Milady climbed the stairs and knocked at the door. A sweet voice called, "Come in."

"Ah, Madame Bonacieux," said Milady sweetly, "I would have known you anywhere. After all that he has told me about you, I recognize you perfectly."

"Who has told you about me?" asked Constance.

"Why, D'Artagnan, of course!"

"D'Artagnan? You have seen him?"

"But of course, my dear child. He is on his way here for you now. He asked me to ride ahead and help you get ready."

"D'Artagnan, coming for me? Oh, how I have dreamed of that for months!"

"He is several hours behind me, so you need not rush, my dear. We shall have time for dinner and a chat."

Their dinner was brought into the room a short time later. Constance was too nervous to eat, but Milady insisted that she would

Milady Brings News of D'Artagnan.

need her strength for the ride back to Paris So she let Milady put a piece of chicken on her plate and pour out some wine for her.

But as Milady poured the wine into Constance's glass, she opened a large ring on he finger and emptied a reddish powder into the wine.

"Come, come!" said Milady, raising he glass. "Do as I do."

Constance, in her excitement, drained he glass along with Milady. Just as they were putting down their glasses, they heard the sound of horses outside the convent.

Constance rose to go to the window, but immediately fell to her knees and turned pale. Milady, however, hurried to the window and recognized the plumed hats and red cloaks of the Musketeers. She turned from the window and rushed out of the room.

"Wait for me," gasped Constance as she tried to drag herself to the door. But she

A Reddish Powder in the Wine

managed to go only a few inches before she sank to the floor, unable to hear her name being called or the sound of boots rushing up the stairs.

D'Artagnan burst into the room followed by his friends. He fell to his knees and lifted the woman he loved in his arms. He covered her face with kisses, but her cold lips did not return them.

Porthos shouted for help at the top of his lungs. Aramis ran to the table to pour some water for the woman. But he was stopped by the sight of Athos standing at the table and gazing with horror at an empty wine glass in his hand.

"Oh God!" cried Athos, lifting his eyes to Heaven. "How could You permit this crime!"

Then he walked slowly to D'Artagnan, who still clung to the lifeless body in his arms. Athos lifted him up gently, and D'Artagnan buried his face in his friend's chest and broke

Another Murder!

into tears.

"My friend," said Athos, "be a man! Women weep for the dead; men avenge them!"

D'Artagnan broke away from Athos and cried, "Then after them! First, Rochefort. Then, Milady."

"No," said Athos, "I shall take care of myself. That vengeance is mine! A husband owes that much to his wife."

Porthos and Aramis looked at Athos, stunned. His wife? But D'Artagnan nodded. Yes, this vengeance did belong to Athos.

D'Artagnan ran down into the courtyard and dragged Rochefort from the carriage. "You murderer!" he screamed. "You shall pay for your crimes!"

And there began the most terrible clashing of swords ever to be seen in the history of France. From the courtyard to the chapel, up the stairs and down, along stone corridors and inside rooms, the two men fought like tigers.

"You Murderer!"

Ten minutes...twenty minutes...thirty minutes...and then Rochefort's sword sliced D'Artagnan's in two. But even this did not stop the enraged Gascon. With the cut-off sword in his hand and murder in his heart, D'Artagnan lunged at Rochefort, sending the stump of the sword into Rochefort's chest and out through his back!

Both men fell—Rochefort, dead and D'Artagnan, gasping for breath. Porthos and Aramis came running to help him.

Meanwhile, Milady, who had been watching this terrible duel from a doorway and waiting for her chance to get out unnoticed, rushed to the carriage. Just as she was about to climb in, she felt a pistol pressed against the back of her head.

"You won't need a carriage where you are going, Milady," said Athos coldly. "I warned you, did I not?"

Milady Won't Need a Carriage.

Athos Returns with a Masked Man.

Chapter 14
The Execution

Athos bound Milady hand and foot and locked her inside the carriage. "Guard her well, my friends!" he said to Porthos, Aramis, and D'Artagnan. "She must not escape us this time. I have some business which will take me away for two hours."

The three men looked at Athos, puzzled, but none would dare question him now.

True to his word, Athos returned two hours later, accompanied by a tall man in a red cloak. A black mask covered his face.

Athos waved for his friends to follow him

with the carriage. They rode in silence for several miles until they reached the bank of a river. There, they stopped and dismounted.

The masked man went to the carriage and dragged Milady to the river bank where the others waited.

"What do you want with me?" she cried to the four men.

"We are here to judge your crimes, Madame," said Athos coldly. "D'Artagnan, you first."

D'Artagnan stepped forward. "I accuse this woman of poisoning Constance Bonacieux and of trying to poison me with wine sent from the Red Dove Inn. God saved me, but another man, a brave guard to the King, died in my place."

Then Porthos stepped forward. "I accuse this woman of arranging the murder of the Duke of Buckingham."

Next came Aramis. "I accuse this woman of

Milady Is Accused.

the death of John Felton, who has been hung because of this fiendish woman."

"Now it is my turn," said Athos, trembling. "I married this woman against the wishes of my family. I gave her my name, my love and my wealth. Then I discovered she was branded."

"You cannot prove the crime for which I was branded," cried Milady. "You cannot find the man who branded me!"

"Silence!" said a voice. "It is my turn."

"Who are you?" cried Milady, as all eyes turned to the masked man.

The man walked in front of Milady and slowly removed his mask.

Milady studied his pale face, hard cold eyes, and smoothly shaven head. Then suddenly, she screamed in terror, "Oh, no, no, no! The executioner of Lille! The man who branded me!"

Athos was as stunned as his friends. He

"The Executioner of Lille!"

knew the man simply as the executioner of this province. He had no idea when he hired him that the man knew Milady.

"Yes, I was once the executioner of Lille," said the man, "and here is my story:

"This woman was once in training to be a nun. The young priest who was instructing her fell under the spell of her beauty and her charm. She managed to lure him away from the church with her promises of love. They had no money when they ran away, so they stole the sacred treasures of the church and sold them. But they were caught and arrested.

"This woman lured her jailer away from his duties and persuaded him to let her escape. But the young priest was sentenced to ten years in prison...and to the branding iron! As the executioner of Lille, I had to brand the guilty man—my brother!

"I swore that this woman should be

Stealing from the Church

punished as well, so I tracked her down and branded her with the same *fleur-de-lis* had put on my brother.

"In the meantime, my brother had escaped from jail, and I was accused of helping him. So I was sentenced to take his place in irons. My brother did not know of this, so he rejoined the woman, and they settled in a small village where they lived as sister and brother while he worked at the church.

"The great lord of the province fell in love with her, and she left the priest to become the rich and titled Countess de la Fère."

All eyes turned to Athos, who nodded that this was the truth

The executioner continued. "My brother could not bear his shame, so he left the village and returned to Lille. When he heard that I was in irons for him, he gave himself up. That very night, he hung himself! These were her crimes. This is why she was

The Young Priest Hung Himself.

branded!"

Athos stepped forward. "Gentlemen, you have heard the crimes this woman has committed. What is your sentence?"

"Death!" said Porthos.

"Death!" said Aramis.

"Death!" said D'Artagnan.

"Death!" said the executioner of Lille.

"And death say I!" said Athos.

Milady uttered a dreadful scream and fell to her knees. The executioner lifted her up and carried her to a small boat tied up on the bank. She kicked and fought, crying out, "You are not my judges! You are murderers!"

Milady's cries were so piercing that they reached D'Artagnan's heart. He started to move towards her when a strong grip on his arm stopped him.

"Take one more step, D'Artagnan," said Athos, "and we cross swords. And this time, I swear to God I'll kill you!"

Athos Warns D'Artagnan.

When the boat reached the opposite shore, the executioner threw his prisoner down on her knees. He raised his great sword above his head, then brought it down with all his strength. A terrible cry echoed across the river as he killed the evil Milady.

The executioner took off his cloak and spread it out on the ground. He placed the remains of the body in it and tied the four corners. Then he tossed the bundle over his shoulder and returned to the boat.

He rowed to the middle of the river and then stopped. He stood up and raised the bundle high above the water. "Let the justice of God be done!" he cried.

And he dropped the bundle into the water and watched as it sank to the bottom.

Four men on the bank removed their hats and said a prayer.

The Execution

D'Artagnan Is Arrested.

Chapter 15
The Four Musketeers

Paris was celebrating the great victory at La Rochelle when D'Artagnan and the Three Musketeers entered the city. As they approached the gates of the palace, they were stopped by a force of the Cardinal's Guards.

"Monsieur D'Artagnan," said the leader, "in the name of His Eminence, I arrest you. We have orders to bring you to the Cardinal immediately."

"Do not fear, my friend," said Athos. "We shall accompany you to Richelieu."

The Guards led D'Artagnan into the

Cardinal's study, but stopped his three friends at the door.

"We shall wait for you, D'Artagnan," said Athos, loud enough for the Cardinal to hear.

D'Artagnan stood facing the Cardinal across a long table. This was his first meeting with Richelieu, and he feared...his last!

"Monsieur," said the Cardinal, "I had hoped one day to hold out my hand in friendship and in praise of your bravery. But I cannot do so now, for you are charged with the murder of a trusted servant of France."

"That woman was guilty of many crimes," said D'Artagnan, "including murder. Not once, but many times over. I only repaid her with a like crime."

"So you did...and Rochefort too. That was quite an accomplishment for a young Gascon. But your victories are too costly, sir, both for me and for France. You shall have to pay for your crimes with your life."

D'Artagnan Is Charged with Murder.

"I think not, Monseigneur," said D'Artagnan with a smile. "For I have a proper warrant for all that a have done."

"A warrant?' asked Richelieu in surprise. "signed by whom?"

"By your Eminence!" said D'Artagnan as he held out the paper which Athos had taken from Milady at the Red Dove Inn.

Richelieu took the paper and read: IT IS BY MY ORDER AND FOR THE GOOD OF FRANCE THAT THE BEARER OF THIS LETTER HAS DONE WHAT HE HAS DONE. 3 DECEMBER 1627. RICHELIEU

After he had finished reading, Richelieu sat in deep thought for several minutes, twisting and untwisting the paper in his hands. Then he looked up and smiled. "One should be more careful of what one puts on paper," he said, tearing the warrant to bits.

Then he picked up his pen and began writing on a large sheet of parchment.

"I am lost!" thought D'Artagnan. "He is

The Cardinal Tears Up the Warrant.

writing my death order. But I shall die bravely!"

"Here, sir," said the Cardinal, handing the parchment to D'Artagnan.

"Why, it's a commission as a lieutenant in the King's Musketeers!" he cried.

"Yes, Monsieur," said the Cardinal. "Simply fill in your name."

"Oh, Monseigneur," cried D'Artagnan, falling to his knees, "I do not deserve such a commission. Serving as a private in the Musketeers would be reward enough for me. I have three friends who are much more worthy of a lieutenant's commission than I am."

"Well, do what you like with it, sir. But remember, it is to you that I give it. Now, good day, Monsieur D'Artagnan."

D'Artagnan left the room in a daze.

"Are you all right, my friend?'a cried Athos as D'Artagnan stumbled through the

D'Artagnan Receives a Commission.

doorway.

"Y-yes," stammered D'Artagnan. "Look, Athos the Cardinal gave me this commission. But I can't take it. It should go to you."

Athos smiled warmly and replied, "My dear friend, this commission is far too much for a common soldier like Athos and far too little for the Count de la Fère. You have earned it. You keep it!"

D'Artagnan pushed the parchment at Porthos "And you, my friend," he said, "just think how splendid you will look in a lieutenant's uniform"

"My dear friend," said Porthos, handing the commission back to D'Artagnan, "I shall soon be wearing the clothing of a nobleman. For my dear duchess has just come into a sizable sum of money. She has been waiting for me for years, and now I shall marry her and take care of her. . . and the money. So keep the lieutenancy. It is not something for

Athos Refuses the Commission.

a nobleman."

"You!" cried D'Artagnan, pushing the commission at Aramis. "You are a man of education, of wisdom. You are far more worthy of this lieutenancy than I am."

My dear friend," said Aramis, "you forget that I am a Musketeer only temporarily. I still plan to join the priesthood when I have the time. No, keep the commission. You will make a brave and daring lieutenant."

"But, my friends," cried D'Artagnan, "if I accept this commission and become an officer I shall lose all my friends. An officer does not have friends."

"Never fear," said Athos as he wrote D'Artagnan's name on the blank line of the parchment. "Even though we are now the Four Musketeers, we shall always be one for all and all for one'"

"Yes!" they shouted together, crossing their four hands, "one for all and all for one!"

"One for All and All for One!"